Razberry Babies
in

The Great
Jam Debate

ISBN: 978-0-9774024-7-2
eBook ISBN: 978-0-9774024-8-9

Book design by UA Design
Names: Spina, Ranee A.

Title: The big jam debate / Ranee A. Spina

Description: 32 pages of color illustrations. / Audience: Ages 3-7. / Summary: Razberry and her furry friends debate which jam flavor is best. Will they figure out a way to stop arguing about which flavor is the favorite?

Identifiers: ISBN 978-0-9774024-7-2 (paperback) / eBook ISBN 978-0-9774024-8-9 (ebook)

Subjects: Girls – Juvenile Fiction. / Problem solving in children – Juvenile Fiction. / Picture Books.

a raz book production, Studio City, CA 91604
Printed in the United States of America
Published November 2023

This story is dedicated to

all those who love

cute, floofy hamsters...

and jam.

One sunny morning,
        as birds chirped
                and flowers bloomed...

Razberry's grandmom had prepared a delicious breakfast,

with jam in many different fruit flavors.

Razberry was a playful girl
with a head full of curls
and a heart full of curiosity.

She had a
magical gift –

Raz could talk
to hamsters!

And on the farm where Raz lived, was a Hamster House!

Home to Nuffster, Taffy, Cassie, and Bandero.

They were always ready

Taffy

Nuffster

for a fun adventure!

Bandero

Cassie

Razberry called to
her furry friends,
"Breakfast time!"

No one knew...

The Great Jam Debate
was about to unfold!

Taffy, Cassie, Bandero and Nuffster held spoons in their tiny paws ready to taste some tasty, fruit jam.

"I love <u>RASPBERRY JAM!</u> It's the best!" exclaimed Raz, reaching for the jam jar of her favorite flavor.

Taffy then said, "I think <u>PEACH JAM</u> is the best!

It's sweet, juicy flavor is simply divine!"

Taffy

Cassie scampered up to
Razberry's shoulder,
"Oh Taffy, you're
simply mistaken!

<u>STRAWBERRY JAM</u> is the
sweetest and tastiest of all!"

She waltzed back down
to her seat singing,
"I love,
    love,
        love it!"

Cassie

Nuffster shouted,
"No way!

BLUEBERRY JAM is the
champion of all jams!

Nuffster

Meanwhile, Bandero sat quietly observing the debate.

A smile formed on his sweet face.

Finally, he spoke in his soft voice, "I... I like classic GRAPE JAM."

Bandero

The debate continued, and their voices grew LOUDER.

The hamsters were trying to convince one another their favorite jam was THE BEST.

It seemed like they would never agree!

Razberry held up her hands to calm the chaos.

"I have an idea.
Let's have a *TASTE TEST* to find out
which jam is truly the best!"

Excitement filled the air as Razberry prepared 5 small dishes of different fruit jams: raspberry, peach, strawberry, blueberry and grape.

Each hamster carefully approached the dishes and took a tiny nibble.

As Taffy tasted the RASPBERRY JAM, she sat up a little taller and thought to herself, "Yum!"

Cassie's eyes widened as she tasted the PEACH JAM. "It's like a little bit of sunshine on my tongue!"

With Bandero's contented sigh, he confirmed his love of GRAPE JAM.

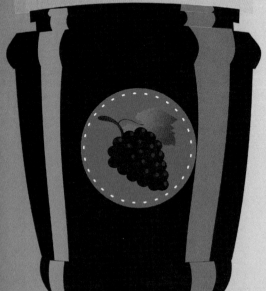

And Nuffster's whiskers twitched in delight with the STRAWBERRY JAM.

Thinking about
the situation,
Razberry declared,

"Why choose one,
when we can enjoy
them ALL!"

The hamsters looked at each other, and realized Raz was right. No need to argue about which jam is the best because...

The best jam is the one shared with friends!

"Blueberry jam is fantastic, but so are the others.

Let's have a JAM-TASTIC feast!"

Nuffster jumped from Razberry's shoulder and did a forward flip down to the table.

They dipped spoons into each jar, spreading jam on their muffins.

A Yummy breakfast was had by all!

From that day on, Razberry and her hamster friends looked forward to their JAM SESSIONS, celebrating all the delightful fruit flavors.

Until next time...